THE MINCE PIE MYSTERY

A SHORT STORY

ALEXANDRIA BLAELOCK

BlueMere Books
MELBOURNE, AUSTRALIA

For permission requests, please contact
enquiries@bluemerebooks.com.

Ordering Information:
Discounts are available on quantity purchases. For details, contact orders@bluemerebooks.com.

The Mince Pie Mystery/Alexandria Blaelock
paperback ISBN: 978-1-925749-50-2
digital ISBN: 978-1-922744-03-6

Book Layout © BookDesignTemplates.com

THE MINCE PIE MYSTERY

Ginger sat at her desk, sipping a lukewarm black coffee while she waited for her boss, Director Edward Weaving, to hang up his phone and call her into his office for their morning meeting.

The sky outside the adjacent window was ridiculously blue, and the hotel tower next door shaded her from the morning sun.

Thankfully, nothing embarrassing to see this morning.

The air-conditioning hadn't evened out yet, and a cascade of cold air fell from the vent above her. Cold enough that not seeing white fog didn't feel right.

She had an overflowing in-tray on her left and a short stack of completed paperwork in the out-tray on her right.

In front of her, resting on her computer keyboard, her daybook enclosed a bunch of papers to go through with Edward.

The lime green panels of her workstation were chosen by the powers that be to reduce anxiety, promote harmony and increase creativity in the office.

Not that she'd dream of telling anyone, but she found it a source of immense satisfaction that the colour provided a striking and attractive contrast to her own.

After all, life is hard enough without clashing with the furniture.

This morning, at any rate, the panels were working on her more or less effectively. Though the day had barely started, and who knew where it was going to end up.

The lopsided tinsel strung up above her desk was already a niggling irritation she could do without, but she couldn't fix it until later in the day without hurting poor Felicity's feelings.

And while other staff had no such qualms, Ginger felt one of her most important roles in the office was to encourage and build up staff morale.

Not just on the Director's behalf, but because happy, confident staff create less drama she'd need to fix up than pessimistic and uncertain ones.

Ginger was the most efficient and effective Personal Assistant in the business, and this had led to her becoming the office's Go-To Girl.

Need toner for the copier? Ask Ginger.

Need a last-minute lunch for your meeting guests? Ask Ginger.

Need a conference for 100 People next week? Ask Ginger.

She'd calmly get it done almost before you'd finished asking.

The funny thing was, next to no one knew Ginger wasn't her real name, and that suited her fine.

Edward nicknamed her Ginger a decade ago when he was one of a team of junior managers she was supporting. He'd asked her one little thing, and fully stressed out by her nemesis Michael Pearce, it'd been the last straw.

She'd exploded in his face, using some "spicy" language to boot.

"Whoa, slow down Ginger," he'd laughed, and never once since called her by her actual name. It was their little joke.

Initially, it was a reminder to take it easy and not stress herself out, but as the years passed, it became more of a recognition of her unflappable professionalism.

As he was prolific in his thanks and praise, there was nothing she wouldn't do for him. She'd become the secret weapon he couldn't do without.

Together they'd become a formidable team, and as he'd skimmed up the corporate ladder, he'd taken her with him.

As she waited, mentally reviewing what she needed to get done, she became aware of a disturbance on the other side of the open-plan office.

Shrill raised voices were disturbing the calm.

Absently, she checked her watch. Nearly ten o'clock.

And as she sat, head tilted to one side to better hear what was going on, she saw the squabbling Data Analysis team approaching like a storm on the horizon.

Or, as they arrived, swooping and screeching around her desk, more like a pack of seagulls fighting over a hot chip.

To be honest, she didn't have the time for this.

Among other things, she was trying to prepare for the board meeting, and she had a stack of papers to print, collate and get in the post by the end of the day.

But it was already too late to escape, and there was no choice but to wait it out.

She hadn't a hope in hell of understanding a word any one of them said, so she let them squawk while she focused her attention on their body language.

Her ability to understand the nub of any given situation wasn't the psychic gift her colleagues thought it was, or something she'd learned, or even a lucky fluke.

It was just the ability to see through the bullshit people said to what they meant, complemented by a deep knowledge of "her" staff developed over time.

Or to put it a simpler way, she could read people.

Little Marguerite in her plain gunmetal grey shift dress clenched her arms like a tyrannosaurus, face red, squeaking in incoherent rage.

Colm, blue jeans and plaid-button down leaned, apparently relaxed, on a supporting pillar gesturing with one hand and interjecting.

Mirella, loose khaki coloured cargo pants and tight rust coloured t-shirt, gestured wildly and stamped her high heeled foot, her usually deep tones rising in pitch as well as volume.

Josh, in turquoise chinos and a mint coloured polo shirt, was a pillar of tightly wound tension with his arms crossed, grunting in agreement.

And poor Felicity, in her cheap pink floral Best and Less shirt-waister dress, wringing her hands, dragged along by the undertow.

Ginger heard Edward call her name, so she stood, smoothing her black, wool crepe suit jacket down around her hips.

"I understand someone has stolen your mince pies. You want to know who, and how they retrieved them from the locked cabinet?"

The five of them nodded in unison.

"I'll look into it," she said, then picked up her daybook and walked into Edward's office, shutting the door behind her.

Aside from glass walls and a door, his workspace was very much like hers. His navy suit jacket hung on a hanger from a hook stuck to the side of one of the filing cabinets along the wall to his left.

"What was that all about?" he asked, rolling up his sleeves.

She sat and opened her notebook as if it was the least important thing on her agenda, as it was, "missing mince pies."

"Do people still leave food in the kitchen and expect it to be there when they get back?"

"I gather these were bought fresh from the market this morning as a midmorning treat for the team meeting, and locked in a cabinet in their corner of the office."

"The mystery of the missing mince pies eh? I look forward to hearing how your investigation goes."

Ginger wrinkled her nose, "I can't imagine how they thought the smell would go undetected.

"Before we get down to business, how's Bronte? I heard you brought her into the office this morning?"

"Ah no, it's nothing serious. Bev and the kids are heading down to the Prom today, and they brought the dog in to say goodbye.

"Oh my god, there was fun all round; she slipped her leash, and the kids were chasing her all around the office."

"I'm sorry I missed it."

"It gets even better - she ran into Michael's office and peed on the carpet. I had to hustle them out of the building before I called Building Services to get a cleaner in to take care of it."

"Then it's lucky he's on leave, or we'd never hear the end of it."

"On my god yes." He held up his crossed fingers, "Hopefully, no one'll tell him."

"How did Bronte get in there? I thought he locked his door when he went away."

"He did, but you remember how he complained his network access keeps dropping out?"

Ginger nodded, she remembered all too well the fuss he'd made about it.

"Well, the IT department sent a technician down this morning to test all the wiring and access points."

"Did they find anything?"

"No, it's just as we suspected, he's an idiot."

"Don't tell me he wasn't plugged in correctly?"

Edward grinned.

"Anyway, how's your mother this morning?"

Ginger signed and scratched an eyebrow with the silver ballpoint pen he'd given her for Christmas several years ago.

"She won't be home for Christmas, which is a shame, but her surgery went well. If she actually does her rehabilitation exercises, she should recover her full range of movement."

"And you doubt that?"

"She says it hurts, so she won't do them. It seems she has some issues with the pain relief, which doesn't help - too much, and she goes to sleep, not enough, and she refuses to move."

"I'm sorry to hear that."

"We'll manage I'm sure. Now, shall we get to business?"

Back at her desk, Ginger stared out of the window and started calculating her suspect pool.

There were usually 52 staff on the floor, but a couple of clicks revealed 19 approved leave applications, leaving 33.

She wrote that down in her daybook, circling 33.

She took the long way around to the kitchen to make more coffee, chatting with people and checking the in/out boards as she went. Another 15 out, left 18, minus herself left 17 staff members.

She crossed out 33 and wrote 17.

Of those, she had four gluten intolerant, two diary allergies, two nut allergies, plus Edward and two others were vegans who were unlikely to steal food of unknown provenance.

That left six suspects, the original complainants plus Hannah.

She crossed out 17 and wrote down the names of her six suspects.

Then she added Edward's wife, kids and dog, IT guy, and cleaner. Another six suspects, for a total of 12 in the mince pie mystery.

Setting the problem aside to simmer for a bit, she focused on organising the board papers, until the potted screen next to her spoke.

"Hi Ginger, how are you?"

She jumped.

"Oh, April!" She clasped a hand to her chest, "have you been here long?"

"Nah, we just started watering on this floor."

"Doing anything nice for Christmas?"

"We're heading down to Rosebud, we've rented a cottage on the beach."

"That sounds wonderful."

"Yes, I'm looking forward to it. This year the days of the public holidays mean we can shut the business down, take a proper break and forget about everything for a week or so."

"The plants are thriving, so you clearly deserve it."

"We're doing a little pruning and cleaning, as well as giving everything a little extra water today because we know the air-con'll be turned off.

"Oh! Thinking of water, did you hear about the Director's dog this morning? Got loose and took a dump in Mr Pearce's office!"

"I heard."

"Couldn't happen to a more deserving man."

Ginger smiled slightly, even outsiders had issues with Michael, "so they say."

"They got a cleaner in, and he was real mad about it."

"I can imagine."

"Anyway, I'd better get on, you have a good Christmas now."

"Thanks, you too."

Ginger added a list of cleared suspects to her daybook, and wrote April's name at the top, noting she'd arrived after the theft was reported.

But her train of thought had derailed, so she decided to take a side trip, and caught an elevator to the basement Building Services office.

"Hi Dianne," she said as she approached the counter, "I heard there was an incident in Mr Pearce's office this morning, and I came down to apologise and thank the cleaner."

"Ginger that's so sweet. I'll go get Bob for you."

Dianne disappeared around the corner, and a moment later, a plump, balding older man in coveralls came out.

"Hi Bob, I just wanted to apologise for—"

"There's no need Ginger, Mrs Weaving already did."

How do you know it was Mrs Weaving? Have you met her before?"

"Nah, I only know it was her because I caught them sneaking out the door to the car park. And when Mr Weaving explained the situation, I put two and two together, and Bob's your uncle, there you have it."

"Nicely done Bob."

He smiled, "I know. Mr Weaving was very embarrassed."

"I can imagine."

"But I have dogs of my own, so I understand, and as long as you get to it quickly, it's not so bad."

"Then we're lucky it was early, and we're lucky it was you."

Bob laughed, "They do say you should always do the worse job first, and you can't get much worse than that!"

"I really hope not!"

"I tell you what though, when I caught the lift back, it smelled like fresh mince pies, and the smell made me want something sweet so bad I had to raid the biscuits when I got back."

He put up a hand to cup his mouth, "don't tell Dianne," he whispered loudly.

Ginger patted his arm, "I'm sure it's all good Bob."

"You know what's even better than that?" he whispered, "my coffee was still warm enough to dunk them in?"

"Really? What time was that then?"

"Can't have been any later than 9:00."

"Well, that's lucky then."

"Yes. I tell you who I feel sorry for," he continued in his usual voice, "I feel sorry for Ivan, he was right there under the desk when the dog let loose. And he was still there when I left."

"That's awful. I must go apologise to him too."

"He didn't seem to be having a good day, so I reckon he'd appreciate that."

"Well, thanks again Bob. Have a great Christmas."

"No worries Ginger, you too."

As she walked away, Ginger wondered if it was a good thing to have cleared five suspects in one swoop.

Seven remaining.

That five of them were the original complainants seemed suspicious.

But she'd focus on the other two; Ivan the IT guy first.

And he was going to be the hardest, because she liked him.

A lot.

She didn't want him to be the thief.

Should he ever invite her out on a date, she'd accept with no hesitation.

And worry about what her mother thought later.

She caught the lift up to his floor, swiped her security card to gain entrance, but stopped by the bathroom first.

After smoothing her hair back with damp hands, and compressing her lips to enhance the colour, she squared her shoulders and walked around the floor to his desk.

"Um. Hi Ivan," she said, cursing herself for turning into an idiot when it counted the most.

She had no problem talking to Chief Executives and politicians, why did an IT guy have to be so difficult.

He pushed his chair away from his desk and jumped to his feet. "Ginger. Erm. Hello. How are you?"

"I'm fine thanks, how are you?"

He scuffed a toe on the carpet, "You look very efficient today."

She smiled, blushing a little, and looked at the floor.

"I just came by to apologise for the dog incident this morning."

His elbow slid off a filing cabinet as he tried to lean nonchalantly on it, "Um, no, it's all good. Mr Weaving already did."

"I know, I just thought... Well, you know."

"I know," he cleared his throat, "I'm sure it would've been easier if Felicity hadn't come past with a box of warm mince pies."

"Felicity? Really? About what time was that then?"

"I'm not exactly sure, say nine-ish."

"Nine-ish. And they came to me about ten."

"Ten? No, I was gone by about nine-thirty."

"Oh, sorry Ivan, I was thinking about something else.

"Were you able to fix Mr Pearce's problem?"

"Oh, no. I think it's just that our broadband access is limited by the facilities supplied by the building owners, and until they upgrade it, we lack the speed and capacity we might get if our offices were somewhere else. Especially as he's surrounded by heavy users and VOIP phones."

"Do you think they'll fix it?"

"Hard to say, but until they do, our security card system is really just a token effort - anyone could walk in or out if they get the timing right."

"That's a worry. Mind you, last year one of the staff let a stranger follow them in, and that person went around and stole a bunch of wallets and phones, so I guess that risk is already there anyway."

"Yes and no - they installed cameras in the lift well on every floor after that, so if your stuff gets stolen, they can check the footage for suspects."

"That's good to know, thanks for share—"

The sound of his name echoed past, and he said, "sorry, that's my boss, I have to go."

"No worries, have a good day."

"Yeah, you too."

He turned away, paused, and then turned back. "Look, Ginger do you want to get a coffee one day?"

She grinned like a madwoman, "I'd love that."

"Great!" His smiled dazzled her as he turned away.

She watched him leave before swiping herself into the grey concrete stairwell, and dancing a little victory dance, punching the air a couple of times as she went.

Only a few seconds later, she heard the alarm system beep and tugged her jacket, hoping she didn't look as stupid as she felt.

"Hi Ginger," said Pete as he raced down the stairs passed her.

"Hi Pete," she called after him and started walking down after him.

"Oh wait," he said and turned and started jogging back up, stopping half a dozen or so steps below her. "Did you hear about Hannah? She was in a car crash last night."

"You're kidding!"

"I wish I was."

"That's awful. Do you know where she is? I'll send some flowers out to her."

"Hold on," he tapped and scrolled his phone, "She's at the Alfred."

"Thanks for letting me know."

"Thanks for organising flowers."

"No worries."

He took a step down, but turned to lean on the balustrade in front of her, looking down the stories to the bottom of the stair.

"Was there something else Pete?"

"Look, I saw something this morning, and I'm not sure what to do about it, and I wonder if you could give me some advice."

"Of course," she said, "tell me what happened."

"Well..."

He paused, then opened his mouth, and paused again.

"If you're not comfortable talking to me, you can always go to HR you know."

"It's not that... Look I'll just spit it out. I was passing through your floor this morning for a meeting with Jess, and I saw Colm abusing Felicity."

"I see."

"I mean I know she's very quiet, and not very good at her job, but I don't think there was any need for him to raise his voice to her. Poor thing ran away crying."

"And where was the rest of the Data Analysis team when this happened?"

"I'm not sure, I passed Marguerite, Mirella and Josh coming back from the kitchen as I went around the corner. They were saying something about looking forward to Christmas treats at their meeting this morning."

"I can't take any official action unless Felicity lodges a complaint, but I'll make a file note with the details. What time did you see this?"

"That was about nine forty-five."

"Nine forty-five, got it."

She took another step down, but still, Pete didn't move.

"Pete?"

"Ginger, while Felicity was running away, I saw him take something from her cabinet and put it in his own."

"You saw him *steal* from her?"

He scrubbed his face with one hand, "I mean it might just have been a stack of notebooks, but what kind of person steals from his colleagues?"

"The wrong kind. Thanks for the information Pete, I'll take care of it."

"Thanks Ginger, you're a legend."

He turned and leapt down the stairs.

She followed at a slower pace, frowning.

This was how she got herself into trouble. Really, she had to stop helping people resolve their own issues.

Not that Colm bullying Felicity was an unusual occurrence. For some reason, he just couldn't leave the girl alone. At this rate, she'd be scarred for life.

Back at her desk, she ordered the flowers, pulled a get well soon card out of her stash, and took it to Alison to start it on a trip around the office for signatures and donations.

"Hannah was in a car crash? But she's such a great driver. You remember when she drove the mini-van to that Christmas barbecue, the oned we had by the Yarra River a couple of years ago?"

"Oh yeah, that's right." Ginger smiled, "When Frank and the engineers sang a million rounds of bottles of beer on the way back."

Alison laughed, "that's right, I'd forgotten."

"That was a good day."

"Yes it was."

Ginger smiled, "okay. I'll leave that with you," and turned away.

"Oh, I saw Ivan here this morning."

She turned back, "yes, he was working in Michael's office."

"I thought I saw him looking for you."

"Oh, I wonder what he wanted. What time was that?"

Alison gave her upper arm a little shove, "I expect he wanted you."

Ginger felt her cheeks grow warm, "don't be so ridiculous."

Alison laughed, "it was about half nine. His phone beeped, and he dropped his tool bag in surprise, and those little screwdrivers they use went everywhere. And then he was crawling around on the floor trying to pick them all up, and Geoffrey nearly fell over him. It was so hilarious. And then he looked at his phone and dashed off.

"You should go see what he wanted."

"Maybe later."

But as she returned to her desk, she felt as though a load had been taken from her shoulders. Alison, inveterate gossip that she was would have mentioned the pies if she'd seen them.

She opened her book and looked at her suspect list.

She moved Hannah and Ivan to the cleared list.

Poor Felicity. Her team hadn't made any effort to make her feel welcome, and she was terrified of them. It was incredible she'd lasted so long. On the one hand, it made perfect sense she'd hide the mince pies from them. On the other, she was still trying to gain their acceptance.

In any case, she was seen leaving the team area at 9:45. At the same time, Marguerite, Mirella and Josh were seen together discussing eating the pies.

That suggested the pies were stolen around 9:45, and the only person in the area was Colm.

Quickly, she needed to see if the pies were where she thought there were, and she needed to do it before anyone left for lunch.

And she needed to take someone with her to the Data Analysis team to witness her actions, so she grabbed Alison on the pretence of taking the card to the other side of the office.

They reached the Data Analysis team space about the same time they did, and they all started talking at the same time.

Ginger held her hand up for silence, and after a few seconds, they quietened down.

"Colm," she said, "may I ask you to open your cabinet."

"I'll do no such thing. Give me a good reason why I should."

"How about proving your innocence."

"I don't know what you mean."

"I mean that you are the only person who had access to the stolen pies, and if you don't want me to take any further action, then you might like to prove you don't have them."

Felicity took a step back as Mirella took a step forward.

"Open the goddamned cupboard dick head."

"I won't," he replied, "you have no call making me feel like a criminal."

Geoffrey walked past, "is that mince pies I can smell, I hope you brought enough for everyone."

"Well," demanded Marguerite, her voice as flat steely as her dress.

Ginger couldn't see her face, but Colm took a step back, as she took one forward.

"For god's sake," Josh said, pushed Colm back into his chair and out of the way before he pulled the doors apart.

And there, on a pack of copy paper, was the box of pies.

Colm collapsed back into himself, "how did you know?"

Ginger drew her eyebrows together, "you were seen bullying Felicity and sending her way in tears, moments before you removed something from her cupboard."

Felicity gasped.

"Presumably you provoked her so she wouldn't think to lock the cupboard before she left.

"But what I don't understand, is what you hoped to achieve by this."

Colm sat up straight in his chair, "it was just a joke, you're making too big a deal of this."

Ginger crossed her arms, "I might agree with you if this situation hadn't been reported to me by a Senior Manager from another department as a bullying incident.

"You're in serious trouble here Colm, there's no option now but to report this as a disciplinary violation.

"You will be counselled, and if your attitude doesn't improve, you face dismissal."

"But it was just a joke!"

"Do you see any of us laughing Colm?" asked Marguerite.

Mirella turned and took Felicity by the arm, "I'm taking Felicity to lunch."

"I'm right behind you," said Josh.

Marguerite grabbed her and Mirella's handbags, "don't bother following us," she said to Colm.

Alison smiled brightly, "that was fun, thanks Colm," and walked away, leaving Ginger in no doubt that it would be all over the office, if not the building by half-past two.

"Enjoy your stolen mince pies Colm," she said, "stolen fruit isn't always the best."

And returned to her own desk.

"Ready for lunch?" Edward asked, shrugging on his jacket.

"Not sure about lunch, but definitely a glass of wine!"

He waited until she'd taken her first sip, then asked, "so how did your investigation go?" "Aahhh," she said, and took a second before putting the glass down.

"Colm provoked an argument with Felicity, and she ran away in tears without locking her cabinet, so he nicked the pies."

"And?"

"And nothing, he said it was a joke."

"Pitiful kind of joke if you ask me."

"I know, and Pete saw it."

"Then we can't let it go this time."

"True, but I don't think Marguerite will let it go. And Alison will make sure no one else does."

"Alison! That's just mean Ginger."

"Two sides mate! Some good's come out of it."

"Some good? Like what."

She counted it off on her fingers, "well, the team's rallied around Felicity, Bob got some sweet biscuits, and I've got a date with Ivan."

"A date eh?"

"A date."

"Well," he said, "looks like the New Year's shaping up just fine."

He lifted his glass, "Merry Christmas, and a Happy New Year."

She clinked hers to his, "And goodwill to all."

THE END

ABOUT THE AUTHOR

Alexandria Blaelock writes stories, some of them for *Ellery Queen's Mystery Magazine* and *Pulphouse Fiction Magazine*. She's also written four self-help books applying business techniques to personal matters like getting dressed, cleaning house, and feeding your friends.

As a recovering Project Manager, she's probably too fond of sticking to plan. She lives in a forest because she enjoys birdsong, the scent of gum leaves and the sun on her face. When not telecommuting to parallel universes from her Melbourne based imagination, she watches K-dramas, talks to animals, and drinks Campari. At the same time.

Discover more at www.alexandriablaelock.com.

OTHER SHORT STORIES BY ALEXANDRIA BLAELOCK

Alma's Grace
Balancing the Book
Bygone Boyfriend
Carmelita Basingstoke
Fate in Your Hands
Kiss of Death
Lady of the Looking Glass
Life in the Security Directorate
Long Weekend in the Snow
Love in the Security Directorate
Morning Star, Evening Star, Superstar
Needy Bitch
Payton's Run
Phoenix Child
Secret Singer
Shining Star
Ship in a Bottle
Simone Says Hands in the Air
The Day the Schedule Broke
The Guardian's Vigil
Toy Soldiers

BOOKS BY ALEXANDRIA BLAELOCK

FICTION

That Love Nonsense

MS BLAELOCK'S BOOKS

Stress Free Dinner Parties
Signature Wardrobe Planning
Holistic Personal Finance
Minimally Viable Housekeeping

www.ingramcontent.com/pod-product-compliance
Lightning Source LLC
Chambersburg PA
CBHW070455170726
48291CB00005B/1768